3

Southern
Mother
Goose

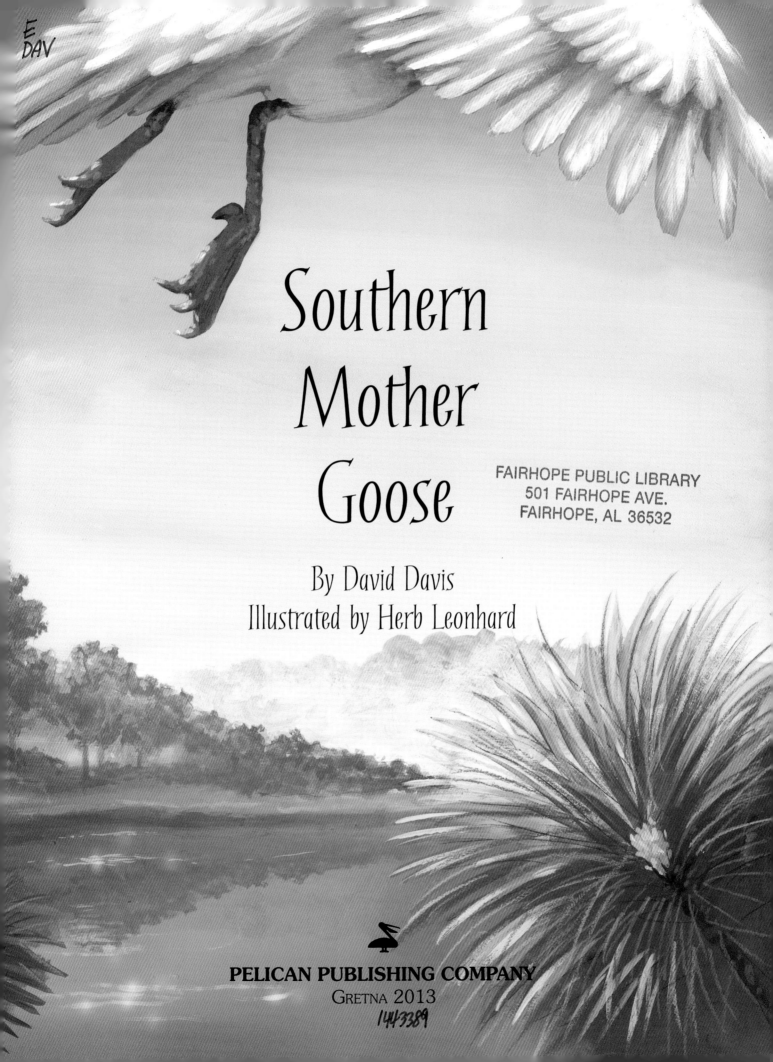

Southern
Mother
Goose

By David Davis

Illustrated by Herb Leonhard

PELICAN PUBLISHING COMPANY

Gretna 2013

For Mark Twain, Jesse Stuart, and Dr. Seuss.
Also, for my editors, Nina Kooij and Abi Pollokoff.—D. D.
For Samuel Clemens and Theodor Geisel.—H. L.

The word "Pelican" and the depiction of a pelican are
trademarks of Pelican Publishing Company, Inc., and are
registered in the U.S. Patent and Trademark Office.

Library of Congress Cataloging-in-Publication Data

Davis, David, 1948 Oct. 29-
  Southern Mother Goose / by David Davis ; illustrated by Herb Leonhard.
    p. cm.
  ISBN 978-1-4556-1760-9 (hardcover : alk. paper) — ISBN 978-1-4556-1761-6 (e-book) 1. Children's poetry, American. 2. Nursery rhymes, American. I. Leonhard, Herb, ill. II. Mother Goose. III. Title.
  PS3554.A93344S686 2013
  811'.54—dc22

                                                2012025153

Printed in Malaysia
Published by Pelican Publishing Company, Inc.
1000 Burmaster Street, Gretna, Louisiana

Mother Goose Flew Way Down South

Mother Goose flew way down South,
Above the swaying pines.
Her magic bird set down his feet,
Where the creeping kudzu winds.
So southern young'uns gather 'round—
She wants to read to you;
Hush, and open both your ears,
'Cause I'm sure she's fixin' to!

Old Auntie Audrey Slept in a Shoe

Old Auntie Audrey slept in a shoe.
She fed forty cats and a dog or two.
The bunch gobbled grits from a big china bowl
And crawled in and out through a hole in the sole.

The cats twitched their tails and licked all of their faces,
While the hounds climbed the leather and chewed on
   the laces.
Old Aunt fetched a quilt and some stockings to sew
And rocked all day long in her chair by the toe.

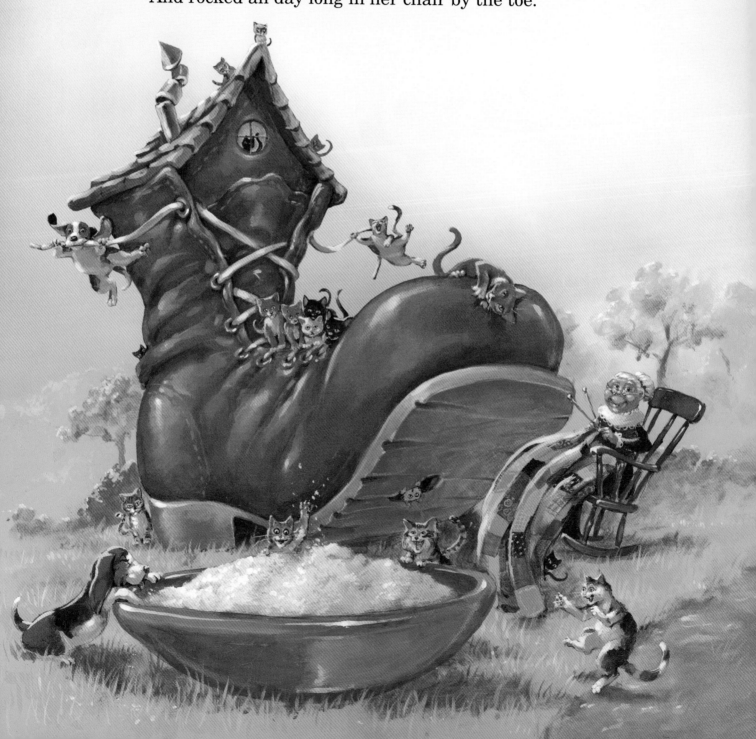

Little Boy Bluegrass

Little Boy Bluegrass
Used to blow on his horn
For the mares in the meadow
And the colts newly born.

But he wanted a paycheck
And life with a thrill,
So he played at the races
In old Louisville.

Rub-a-Dub-Dub

Rub-a-dub-dub!
Crawfish in a tub,
Bathing and splashing away.
But one yelled, "Mon Dieu,
I smell rice and a roux!
We're part of a big étouffée!"

Little Miss Muffet

Little Miss Muffet,
On a small 'Bama tuffet,
Didn't like curds and whey.
So she squealed, "I declare,
I'll tease my big hair
And dine in a roadside café."

Old Mother Hubbard

Old Mother Hubbard
Opened the cupboard
To get her hound dog a bone.
She spied cornbread there,
Sat down in her chair—
Fido didn't favor corn pone.

So she picked black-eyed peas
To cook for him later,
But he whimpered a bit
And howled for a 'tater.

She marched to the market
And bought him a yam,
But he turned up his nose,
'Cause that hound wanted ham.

She baked him a biscuit
And a juicy hog jowl,
But he sniffed at his dish
And started to growl.

She dropped by the dairy
To fetch him some butter,
But when she got back,
The dog gave a shudder.

She crossed both her arms,
Set the grub on the shelf,
Yelled, "Hound, if you're hungry,
Fetch the food for yourself!"

Every Star in Tennessee

Every star in Tennessee
Shines above my bed and me.
I try to count them in the night
When Ma and Pa turn out the light,
But before I get to ten,
I always fall asleep again.

The Texas Range

The Texas Range is big and wide
Where longhorns moo and Rangers ride.
Cowboys camp 'neath the setting sun,
While bobwhites call and coyotes run.

Cowpokes at rest, un-fenced and free,
In the thorny shade of a mesquite tree;
They prop their boots in a campfire's light,
And watch the stars in the Texas night.

Hickory Dickory Dock

Hickory Dickory Dock,
Mules toted Papaw's clock.
They brayed and kicked
Each time it ticked,
Hickory Dickory Dock.

A Monstrous Mississippi Mosquito

A monstrous Mississippi mosquito
Munched on a giant burrito.
He clutched in his mitts
Some peaches and grits,
A dill pickle, and a fried green tomato.

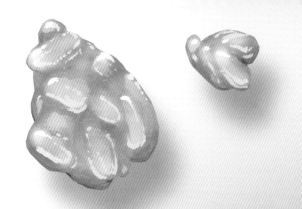

Peter, Peter, Praline-Eater

Peter, Peter, praline-eater,
Got a gal and ran to greet her.
They made a lunch in New Orleans
Of sugarcane and sweet pralines.

Catahoula Dogs and Calico Cats

Catahoula Dogs and Calico Cats
Stroll Beale Street in Panama hats.
In dark sun shades and pin-striped suits,
They play hot blues and tap their boots.
When friendly folks toss them a tip,
They wag their tails and do a flip.

Yankee Doodle Came Down South

Yankee Doodle came down South,
Riding on a pony.
Now, he eats his catfish fried—
No cheese-steaks or baloney.

Yankee Doodle stayed down South
And traded in his pony.
Now, he fills his pickup truck
With grits, not macaroni!

Sassy Sue in Scarlet Jeans

Sassy Sue in scarlet jeans
Stirred sorghum syrup in her greens.
She said, "This stuff seems more appealing
When it sticks to sister's ceiling."

Jack and Jill in Alabama

Jack and Jill jogged up the hill
To see the stock car races.
They climbed the giant grandstand
And settled in their places.

Jill and Jack jogged down the hill
And asked when they got back,
"How come the drivers just turn left
At the Talladega track?"

Four and Twenty Turkeys

Four and twenty turkeys
Baked into a pie
Were so big and heavy,
It made the waiters cry.

Four and twenty turkeys
All began to gobble,
"See those silly servers strain,
And watch them weep and wobble!"

Humpty Dumpty Rolled to Arkansas

Humpty rolled to Arkansas,
Climbed a fence with his Maw and Paw.
A gray mule kicked those three eggs down—
They broke and splattered on the ground!

The farmer's cat and barnyard hen
Patched up Humpty and his folks again.
See them sleepin' in the yeller hay?
Scrambled egg yokels to this day.

A Georgia Gal Picking Peaches

A Georgia gal out picking peaches
Tastes every one that her arm reaches.
She ate so many that I hear tell,
One isn't left for her to sell.

Hickety Pickety, My Texas Hen

Hickety Pickety, my Texas hen,
Lays hot tamales in her pen.
She lays a dozen every day,
Then dances 'round and clucks, "Olé!"

A Pirate from South Carolina

A pirate from South Carolina,
Navigated his ship with a Myna,
When the bird squawked, "Turn here,"
The directions weren't clear,
And they ended up sailing to China.

Boyd and Ben

Boyd and Ben kick up their heels
And clog dance to Virginia reels.
So shuck your cares and grab a dollar,
Let's ride the train to Possum Holler!

They'll fiddle high and fiddle low
And pick a tune on the old banjo.
When we wave goodbye to Boyd and Ben,
They smile and say, "Come back, again!"

Mississippi Steamboat

Mississippi steamboat
Rounds the bend
Down Natchez way
And back again.

Mississippi steamboat,
Floating free,
Why don't you stop,
And pick up me?

Jack Sprat and His Missus

Jack Sprat and his Missus
Boiled okra in tureens.
They spilled it on the sidewalk
And slid down to New Orleans.

Virginia Mice Set Sail One Week

Virginia mice set sail one week
Across the bay called Chesapeake.
They anchored there and fished all day
And ate Swiss cheese off a silver tray.
In moonlit night they made for shore;
That's all there is—there ain't no more.

Miami Mary, Quite Contrary

Miami Mary, quite contrary,
How does your garden grow?
"I'm out of reach
While at the beach,
So, really, I don't know."

Georgie Porgie from Pontchartrain

Georgie Porgie from Pontchartrain
Kissed all the girls at Old Tulane.
Then he knew just what to do:
He kissed the girls at LSU!

There's a Mountain Trail in Tennessee

There's a mountain trail in Tennessee
Meant for folks like you and me.
Let's hike above the world so high
And touch the clouds as they roll by.

We'll shuck our shoes where soft fern grows;
In singing springs we'll dip our toes.
There's just one place for you and me:
The mountain views of Tennessee.

Old King Cajun

Old King Cajun
Was a sight when ragin',
A sight when ragin' was he!
He called for his chips,
And he called for his dips,
And he called for his TV sets three.

He watched Louisiana football all day long
And yelled and screamed
If a coach guessed wrong.

Boiled Peanuts by the Sea

South Carolina is the place to be
For boiled peanuts by the sea,
So a northern judge and a southern boy
Bought two big bags and dined with joy.
While wolfing down a pound or two,
The judge spied hulls by the boy's shoe.
The boy yelled; the man's face fell:
"You're not supposed to eat the shell!"

Pat-a-cake, Pat-a-cake, in Old Kentucky

Pat-a-cake, pat-a-cake,
In old Kentucky,
Make up a pancake
For me and Bucky,
Flip it, and turn it, and butter it there;
We're going to Paducah,
To the County Fair.

A Virginia Farmer Named Kent

A Virginia farmer named Kent
Owns a slanty old farmhouse that's bent.
Though he slides out of bed
And sometimes bumps his head,
Since the place is all his, he's content.

Charlie Chester Chased a Chimp in Chattahoochee

Charlie Chester chased a chimp in Chattahoochee,
A chimp in Chattahoochee Charlie Chester chased.
If Charlie Chester chased a chimp in Chattahoochee,
Where's the chimp in Chattahoochee Charlie Chester
    chased?

A Texas Cow and a Georgia Cat

A Texas cow and a Georgia cat
Do-si-doed 'round a pork pie hat.
The cat meowed and swished her tail
While lapping cream from the milking pail.

The crooning cow danced an old soft-shoe
And clicked her hooves with every moo.
A blue tick hound by the barnyard wall
Howled harmony in a southern drawl.

A Billy Goat That Followed Me

A billy goat that followed me
Ate all the grass in Tennessee.
He ate Pa's shoes and Mama's rings;
He munched my mattress—and the springs.

He chewed the rug on Mama's floor
And chomped the rubber 'round the door.
He ripped the paper off the wall
And bit the boards along the hall.

He slurped my sweater and my hat
And chewed the tail-fur off our cat.
He cropped the flowers in the yard
Then licked up twenty pounds of lard.

His tastes are weird, without a doubt—
He'll even eat a Brussels sprout!
If you want him, take him free,
'Cause he's so hungry—he might eat me!

My Big Feet

My feet are way too big for me—
They're all I need to water ski.
But Mama says I'm like a pup:
They'll fit me fine when I grow up.

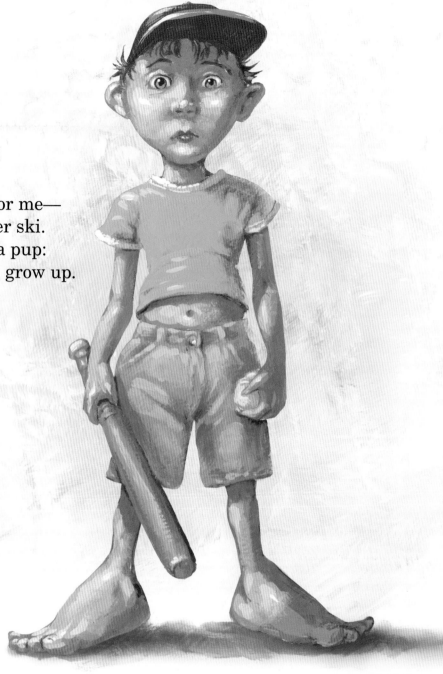

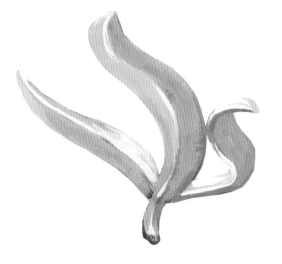

Hal and Hank and Little Hannah

Hal and Hank and little Hannah
Ride bananas through Savannah.
They slick the peels beneath their sled
And slide downtown, I hear it said.
The city slickers scream and sigh,
"Bananas should be in a pie!"

Southern Grits and Butter

Northern folks like their grits sweet—
They figure grits are Cream of Wheat—
But southern folks pitch wall-eyed fits
If you spoon sugar on their grits.
So don't give Pa a breakfast shudder:
Serve him grits with golden butter.

Uncle Fudd's Hog

The hog that's owned by Uncle Fudd
Roots and rolls 'round in the mud.
Fill his trough a time or two,
And he'll squeal a bit for you.

A Walk in Florida

Let's walk barefoot in Florida sand
And snatch a snack we'll pick by hand.
I'll pluck sweet fruit from a citrus tree,
One orange for you—and two for me!

Jack's Not Nimble

Jack's not nimble,
Jack's not quick.
That boy won't work
Or hit a lick.

If he won't stir,
One thing is true:
Jack's sure to miss
A meal or two.

Southpaw Simon, Slick, and Wyman

Southpaw Simon, Slick, and Wyman,
Stopped at a country store.
Ole Southpaw Simon
(A real Moon Pie man)
Ate three and asked for more.
He guzzled down a cold R.C.
Then grinned and asked, "Are these snacks free?"

Hey Diddle Diddle

Hey diddle diddle,
Old banjo and fiddle,
A mountain guitar, and dobro
Played bluegrass at night
But didn't sound right,
So a mandolin joined in the show.

Collard, Turnip, and Mustard Greens

Collard, turnip, and mustard greens,
Each southern child knows what that means.
Mamaw cooks them for us all,
So dip a plate and eat some, y'all!

An Ole Miss Fast Talker

An Ole Miss fast talker,
While reading his Faulkner,
Munched on an Oxford fried pie.
He scribbled a note,
Then read what he wrote,
And said, "Just like William am I!"

Let's Go Swimming

Hey, you young'uns, let's go swimming
With Maw and Paw and Grandpaw Fleming,
Grab Sis and Sue and brother Paul
And tire tubes—enough for all!

Come splash and float around the creek,
Play water tag and hide and seek,
When day is done without a doubt,
We'll fall asleep—we're plumb wore out!

It's Time to Sleep

The southern stars
Bright in the sky
Tell Mother Goose
It's time to fly.

So little young'uns,
Rest your heads
On fluffy pillows
In feather beds.

You're soon to sleep,
So wave goodbye
To the smiling moon
In the purple sky.

Please, listen close
While shadows fall;
Hear Mother's Goose
Honk, "Good night, y'all."